Extreme Bicycle Stunt Riding Moves

By Danny Parr

Consultant:
Moniqua Plante
Assistant Director of Marketing
ESPN X Games

CAPSTONE
HIGH-INTEREST
BOOKS

an imprint of Capstone Press
Mankato, Minnesota

Capstone High-Interest Books are published by Capstone Press
151 Good Counsel Drive, P.O. Box 669, Mankato, Minnesota 56002
http://www.capstone-press.com

Library of Congress Cataloging-in-Publication Data
Parr, Danny.
    Extreme bicycle stunt riding moves/by Danny Parr.
    p.cm.—(Behind the Moves)
    Includes bibliographical references (p. 31) and index.
    ISBN 0-7368-0781-0
1. Bicycle motocross—Juvenile literature. 2. Stunt cycling—Juvenile literature.
[1. Bicycle motocross. 2. Stunt cycling. 3. Extreme sports.] I. Title. II. Series.
GV1049.3.P37 2001
796.6—dc21   00-009811

Summary: Discusses the sport of extreme bicycle stunt riding, including the
moves involved in the sport.

Editorial Credits
Angela Kaelberer, editor; Karen Risch, product planning editor; Kia Bielke,
    cover designer and illustrator; Katy Kudela, photo researcher

Photo Credits
Allsport USA/Tom Hauck, 20
Gene Lower/Slingshot Photography, cover, 4, 6, 8, 12, 19, 21 (top), 22, 29
Mark Turner, 26 (inset)
Shazamm, 7 (bottom), 10, 13, 15, 18, 21 (bottom), 24 (top), 24 (bottom)
SportsChrome-USA/Rob Tringali, Jr., 4 (inset), 7 (top), 10 (inset), 16 (inset),
    26; Michael Zito, 16

1 2 3 4 5 6 06 05 04 03 02 01

Table of Contents

Vert riders perform stunts off ramps.

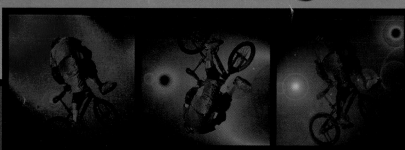

Learn about:

- *BMX history*

- *Types of stunt riding*

- *Frames and equipment*

Extreme Bicycle Stunt Riding

In the 1970s, people began racing small motorcycles on dirt tracks. This sport is called motocross.

Bicycle riders watched the motocross riders performing jumps and stunts on their motorcycles. The bicycle riders wanted to try these stunts. They changed their bikes to make them better for dirt track riding.

The new bikes had smaller, more lightweight frames than street bikes. Riders also put wide tires on the bikes. The tires had a great deal of tread. These bumps and deep grooves gripped the dirt tracks better than regular bike tires did.

Riders began racing these bikes on dirt tracks. They called their new sport "bicycle motocross." Riders soon shortened this name to BMX.

Flatland riders perform stunts on level ground.

A New Sport

Many BMX riders also are skateboarders. By 1976, these riders created a new sport. This sport combined BMX bikes with skateboard stunts. They called this new sport "BMX freestyle." Today, most people call it freestyle bicycle stunt riding.

The sport's popularity increased in 1995. That year, the ESPN TV network started an extreme sports competition called the X Games. This competition includes freestyle bicycle stunt riding.

Types of Bicycle Stunt Riding

Four types of bicycle stunt riding exist. They are dirt, flatland, street, and vert riding.

Dirt riders perform stunts off dirt mounds. These mounds often are at the bottom of hills.

Flatland riders perform stunts on level ground such as paved parking lots. Flatland riders balance on the bike's pedals, seat, axle pegs, or handlebars as they perform stunts.

Street or park riders perform stunts on obstacles such as buildings, curbs, and stair railings. Many street riders perform stunts in skateboard parks or on courses built for stunt riding. These courses are called park courses.

Vert riders perform stunts on large wooden ramps. These ramps can either be half-pipe or quarter-pipe ramps.

Dirt riders perform stunts off mounds of dirt.

Street riders perform stunts on park courses.

7

Ramps

Half-pipe ramps also are called "vert ramps." They have two curved walls connected by a flat area. The curved parts of the walls are called transitions. Most half-pipes are 10 to 12 feet (3 to 3.7 meters) high. Riders speed up the walls and perform multiple stunts in the air. Most half-pipe ramps have a metal bar called a

Riders perform stunts on ramp copings.

coping at the top. Vert riders perform stunts on the coping.

Quarter-pipe ramps have only one curved wall. Some riders speed up the ramp and jump off it. Others turn around in the air and ride down the ramp. Riders perform stunts as they move through the air. Most quarter-pipe ramps are 6 to 8 feet (1.8 to 2.4 meters) high.

Frames and Equipment

Most stunt bike frames are made of chromoly steel alloy. This material is a mixture of two metals called chromium and molybdenum. "CrMo" bikes are heavy and strong. They weigh as much as 35 pounds (16 kilograms).

Some stunt bikes have extra equipment. Riders often put metal pegs on the axles of their bike wheels. These pegs are 3 to 4 inches (7.6 to 10 centimeters) long. Flatland riders balance on the pegs as they perform stunts. Street and vert riders use the pegs to slide across obstacles. Obstacles can include railings, copings, and cement curbs or benches. Many flatland bikes also have a standing platform in front of the seat. Flatland riders sometimes balance on this platform during stunts.

Many flatland riders perform endos.

Learn about:

■ **Endos and manuals**

■ **Hitchhikers**

■ **Tailwhips and whiplashes**

Chapter Two

Flatland Stunts

Flatland riders perform most of their stunts by balancing on their bikes. They link several stunts together. Flatland stunts require a great deal of balance and technical skill.

Many flatland riders perform endos. Riders roll their bikes forward to begin an endo. They put their feet down or lock the front brake to stop the bike. Riders push forward on the handlebars. They throw their weight to the front of the bike. This lifts the back wheel off the ground. Riders balance on the front wheel for several seconds. They then rock backward to drop the back wheel to the ground.

A manual pushes the front wheel off the ground.

Manuals and Hitchhikers

Riders stand on the pedals to begin a manual. They pull up on the handlebars and push their body back. This action pulls the front wheel off the ground.

Riders balance on the pedals with the front wheel 12 to 18 inches (30 to 46 centimeters) off the ground. They move their knees to keep the bike rolling on the back wheel. They balance this way for several seconds without pedaling. Riders sometimes stand on the bike's rear pegs as they perform manuals.

Flatland riders also perform hitchhikers. A rider begins a hitchhiker by rolling the bike on the front wheel. The rider's feet are on the front pegs. The rider holds the rear tire almost straight up in the air. The handlebars almost brush the ground.

The rear tire points up during a hitchhiker.

Tailwhips and Whiplashes

Flatland and street riders perform some of the same stunts. One of these stunts is the tailwhip.

Flatland riders begin the tailwhip with their feet on the pedals. They balance on the front wheel. Riders then jump off the pedals. They rotate the bike frame around the handlebars' axis. They then land with their feet back on the pedals.

Street and vert riders perform tailwhips while in the air. Riders rotate the bike's frame around the handlebars' axis. As they do this, they hold their bodies and the handlebars still. They land back on the bike before it hits the ground.

Flatland riders perform their own version of a tailwhip while balancing on the pegs. This stunt is called a whiplash. Riders put one foot on the front peg. They put the other foot on the back peg on the same side. They rotate the bike around the handlebars' axis while lifting their feet off the pegs. Riders then walk around their bikes by switching their feet from one peg to the next. They slowly roll the bikes across the ground as they walk. They finish the stunt by putting one foot up on the frame.

Riders use the pegs to perform a whiplash.

Street riders perform bunny hops.

Learn about:

Bunny hops and grinds

Spins and flips

No handers, no footers, and Supermans

Chapter Three

Street and Vert Stunts

Street riding is the oldest type of bicycle stunt riding. Riders first performed street stunts on obstacles found on streets and sidewalks.

Today, many cities do not allow bicycle stunt riding on their streets. Many street riders now ride at skateboard parks or on bicycle stunt courses.

Bunny Hops

Riders sometimes lift both wheels off the ground at the same time. This stunt is called a bunny hop. Riders often perform bunny hops to get their bikes up on obstacles.

Riders perform bunny hops by lifting their weight off the seat. They point their toes down to pull the pedals back and upward. At the same time, they pull up on the handlebars. Both wheels lift up and then bounce down.

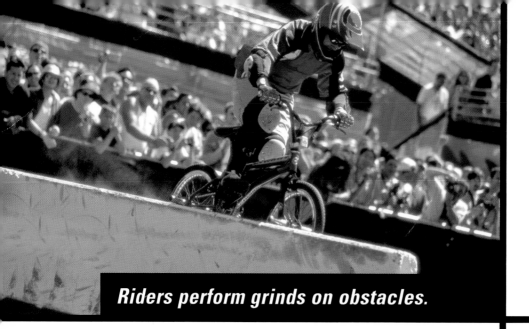

Riders perform grinds on obstacles.

Grinds

A grind involves sliding the frame or the pegs along a ramp's coping or an obstacle's edge. Riders sometimes perform grinds in combination with other tricks.

Some grinds also use the wheels. To perform a feeble grind, riders roll on the front wheel. The rear peg slides across the obstacle.

Spins and Flips

Vert riders perform some street stunts such as grinds. But most vert stunts are aerials. Riders perform these stunts as high as 15 feet (4.6 meters) above the ramp.

Spins are aerial stunts. A half spin is called a 180. A full spin is called a 360. Experienced riders perform 540, 720, and even 900 spins. Riders spin two-and-a-half times in the air during a 900.

Riders also perform flips in the air. To perform a flip, riders lean back on their bikes as they ride up the ramp. They then perform a backward somersault in the air before landing backward or "fakie" on the ramp.

A flip looks like a somersault in the air.

Riders swing their legs during a no footer.

No Handers and No Footers

Riders sometimes take their feet or hands off the bike as they perform stunts. Some riders take one hand off the handlebars or one foot off the pedals. Others perform more daring stunts.

To perform a no hander, riders stand up on the pedals when they are in the air. They pinch the seat between their knees and hold tight to keep the bike steady. They swing their hands behind their back when they reach the highest point in the air. Riders put their hands back on the handlebars as they start to come down.

To perform a no footer, riders lift their feet off the pedals. They swing their legs wide apart. They then return their feet to the pedals.

Some experienced riders perform nothings. This stunt is a no hander and a no footer performed at the same time. This stunt requires a great deal of skill.

No hander

A nothing requires a great deal of skill.

Riders and fans enjoy the Superman seat-grab.

Superman

The Superman is a favorite stunt of both riders and fans. Riders take both feet off the pedals when they are in the air. They kick their feet out behind them without letting go of the handlebars. Riders make themselves as flat as possible. They look like the comic book character Superman as he flies. Riders put their feet back on the pedals as they start to come down.

Many riders perform a form of the Superman called a Superman seat-grab. During the stunt, the rider places one hand on the bike's seat.

Extreme Bicycle Stunt Riding Slang

air—a jump performed off a ramp

bail—to jump off the bike to avoid a crash

brain bucket—a bike helmet

catch air—to go high in the air during a jump

chew—to crash

flatbottom—the flat area between a half-pipe ramp's transitions

loop—a backflip

pump—to ride at a fast, even rate in order to increase speed on ramp stunts

showboat—to show off while riding or doing stunts

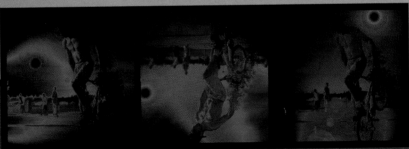

Learn about:

- **Safety equipment**
- **Safe riding**
- **Learning to fall**

Chapter Four

Safety

Bicycle stunt riding is dangerous. But riders who follow safety rules usually have longer riding careers than those who do not. These safe riders may be able to learn more difficult stunts.

Safety Equipment

A good helmet is a bicycle stunt rider's most important piece of safety equipment. Most riders wear full head helmets that curve around their face and cover their chin. Some helmets have visors. These clear shields protect the rider's face and eyes from the sun. Many riders also wear goggles or other protective eye gear.

Other safety equipment protects riders' bodies. All riders should wear elbow pads and knee pads. This padding protects riders from bruises, scrapes, and broken bones. Riders wear knee braces to protect their knees from crashes. Riders also wear gloves to protect their hands and help them grip the handlebars.

Safe Riding

Most stunt riders practice stunts with at least one other rider. One rider can help if the other gets hurt while practicing a stunt.

Knowing how to fall can prevent a rider from being hurt. Beginning riders should practice falling on a soft surface such as grass.

Most stunt riders begin with flatland stunts. Many flatland stunts are easier to learn than other stunts. Flatland stunts also usually are safer than other stunts. They do not involve jumps. Because of this, many professional flatland riders do not wear helmets. But beginning flatland riders should always wear protective gear.

As riders improve, they can learn other types of stunts. Vert stunts are the most difficult and dangerous. Only experienced riders should try these stunts.

Bicycle stunt riders work to make their sport better and more interesting. They know that safe riders will be able to continue to compete and invent new stunts. These riders will help to improve the sport in the future.

Helmets, padding, and gloves protect riders.

Words to Know

aerial (AIR-ee-uhl)—a stunt performed in the air

axis (AK-siss)—the part of the handlebars that attaches to the bike's frame

axle (AK-suhl)—a rod in the center of the wheel; the wheel turns around the axle.

chromoly (KROH-muh-lee)—a mixture of two metals called chromium and molybdenum; this material also is called "CrMo."

coping (KO-ping)—a metal bar at the top edge of a ramp or a cement edge such as the edge of a swimming pool; riders perform stunts on copings.

obstacle (OB-stuh-kuhl)—an object that stands in a rider's way; riders often perform stunts on obstacles.

transition (tran-ZISH-uhn)—the curve of a ramp between the flat area and the walls

visor (VYE-zur)—a clear shield on the front of a bike helmet

To Learn More

Glaser, Jason. *Bicycle Stunt Riding.* Extreme Sports. Mankato, Minn.: Capstone High-Interest Books, 1999.

Hayhurst, Chris. *Bicycle Stunt Riding!: Catch Air.* The Extreme Sports Collection. New York: Rosen Central, 2000.

Koeppel, Dan. *The Extreme Sports Almanac.* Los Angeles: Lowell House Juvenile, 1998.

Useful Addresses

American Bicycle Association
P.O. Box 718
Chandler, AZ 85244

Canadian BMX Association
P.O. Box 2080
Grand Forks, BC V0H 1H0
Canada

USA Cycling
One Olympic Plaza
Colorado Springs, CO 80909-5775

Internet Sites

Canadian BMX Association Track Guide

http://www.bmxracing.net/canadabmxtracks.html

ESPN.com—Extreme Sports

http://espn.go.com/extreme

National Bicycle League

http://www.nbl.org/Mainframe.htm

Ride BMX

http://www.bmxonline.com/ride

Index